A Prayer To A Goddess

LIANA BROOKS

OTHER WORKS

ALL I WANT FOR CHRISTMAS

All I Want For Christmas Is A Reaper
All I Want For Christmas Is A Werewolf

FLEET OF MALIK

Bodies In Motion
Change of Momentum

HEROES AND VILLAINS

Even Villains Fall In Love
Even Villains Go To The Movies
Even Villains Have Interns
Even Villains Play The Hero (books 1 – 3 omnibus)
The Polar Terror

TIME AND SHADOWS

The Day Before
Convergence Point
Decoherence

SHORTER WORKS

Fey Lights
Prime Sensations
Darkness and Good

Find other works by the author at
www.lianabrooks.com

A Prayer To A Goddess

INKLET #95

LIANA BROOKS

Inkprint PRESS

www.inkprintpress.com

Print ISBN: 978-1-922434-35-7
eBook ISBN: 9781393279785

www.inkprintpress.com

National Library of Australia Cataloguing-in-Publication Data
Brooks, Liana 1982 –
A Prayer To A Goddess
58 p.
ISBN: 978-1-922434-35-7
Inkprint Press, Canberra, Australia
1. Fiction—Fantasy—Epic 2. Fiction—Fantasy—
Romance 3. Fiction—Short Stories

First Print Edition: December 2022
Cover photo © cokacoka via Deposit Photos
Cover design © Inkprint Press
Interior art © Amy Laurens

PRAYER TO A GODDESS

"OH, GODDESS! OH, GODDESS!"

The cry echoed through my house too loud to ignore.

I tried. I sunk myself in my giant copper bathtub and tried to ignore the voice begging for my attention. But it was hard.

Prayers from the faithful rarely broke the barriers between the mortal and celestial realm. When I was near people I could hear their thoughts, know their wants and needs, with almost no effort at all. Even a faithless atheist was an open book to me if I touched them. But, safely cocooned in a world of magic, the only thoughts and prayers I heard were those backed by passionate faith.

Strong emotions like fear and hope made prayers clear even here.

"Oh, Goddess, I need you!" A man's voice, strong and clear and begging.

Rolling my eyes, I climbed out of the bath, dried off, and wrapped a diaphanous garnet robe around me. My followers were not particularly devout as a rule and had no expectation of me manifesting looking a certain way. I was a goddess of a city—a small village when I was young—and my godhood was tied to the city, not to a set of religious dictates, although I'd laid down a few ground rules early on. I was not manifesting for every stubbed toe, hurt feelings, or missing ox.

I stepped forward, out of the celestial realm and into the penitent's hour of great need…

…amid the smell of cheap incense, second-hand wine, and the dark, smoke-choked rooms of a place with bad music and yelling downstairs and procreation next door.

And a very, very naked man who was standing fully erect in every sense of the word, arms outstretched toward me.

"Oh, dear Me!" I spun around trying to get *that* image out of my head.

There was a buxom woman on the bed, long tan legs and chestnut hair piled into ringlets, clutching at badly dyed red sheets and staring wide-eyed at me.

"Did you pray for me?" I asked the girl. That almost made sense. "Is he attacking you?"

She shook her head in a tiny, fearful 'No'.

Regretting godhood, I turned to the amorous young man. He had dark brown, curly hair that was common in my city and the healthy look of someone who worked out under the sun for a living. "Did you pray for me?"

"Um..." He pressed his lips together guiltily and glanced at the woman in the bed.

"Did you passionately blaspheme my name while hoping to have sex with her?"

He had. This idiot had really called out to his goddess in the throes of passion.

I covered my eyes. "This is why I let you have plagues," I muttered. "Cuts down on idiots."

"Goddess, forgive me." He didn't wilt or bow, but he had a charming smile. "I have had faith in you since my youth. Your name is on my lips daily in prayer."

"This isn't prayer!" I refrained from

killing him with a thought. I could do it, but it wasn't the sort of thing I wanted to get into the habit of doing. Burn one annoying supplicant and pretty soon you have an entire army of cultish lunatics burning cities in your name. It happened to another immortal I knew and the whole business was just ugly. Plus, it's a lot of work. "This is blasphemy. Remember? The edicts of the Goddess say what? Do not call upon the Goddess..."

"...in thoughtless moments," the boy finished.

"Right!" Blessed be My name.

He licked his lips. "I... ah... apologize?"

I nodded.

The young man looked at his lusty companion and back at me. "Would—would you like to stay? You could join us, I suppose, since you're here?"

Oh, dear Me in heaven. "No, thank you, small pricks in a flea-infested bed are not my definition of a good time. But, by all means, sex away." I turned to the woman. "You are consenting to this, correct?"

"Oh, um, yes… Goddess?"

"Yes, I am the Goddess of this city," I confirmed. Her thoughts were barely a whisper so she was either new to the city or raised in a faithless household. I really didn't care. "Very well, I leave my blessing upon you both. You will enjoy consensual sex without worries of pregnancy or disease until you call upon my name to bless your bridal bed." I gave the girl a once over. "And you in particular I bless with freedom from all the pains of womanhood until you call upon me to restore your womb and bless you with fertility."

She frowned in confusion for a moment and then her smile brightened. "Really?"

"Yes, the advantages of having a Goddess and not a God. I know what women need. As for you," I rounded on my faithful supplicant, "do not call for me in the bedchamber again, you naked nit!" I smacked him (lightly) upside the head. Some people wish they could knock sense into people; I could actually do it.

I stepped away from the brothel, wondering if a few more hits wouldn't be required to get that particular young man to be sensible.

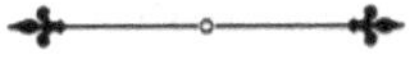

"Goddess! Oh, Goddess! Ever merciful and always listening, GODDESS!!!"

Gods weren't supposed to physically cringe when we heard someone pray. I'm sure I'd heard that somewhere.

I wasn't born to godhood. There's no school for it. No organized ranks of god-dom. We all come to it differently and figure it out on our own.

In my case, when the village along the river Krath was young and the far side of the river was covered in old, thick woods full of monsters, the people would sometimes take someone to feed to those monsters.

At age fourteen or so I was chosen. Apparently by the Elder Gods, or so the leader of the village proclaimed after seeing a row of freckles on my hip that looked like a constellation of stars. When the village leader had seen my freckles was one of those questions I will forever wonder about, because he died long before I thought to ask. But, old perv or not, he convinced everyone that I was Chosen and that by throwing me across the river the village would be saved.

And it was.

Because it had been a dry summer and I accidentally set the forest on fire, thus burning it down and killing all the bandits who were the only monsters lurking under those ancient, highly-flammable boughs.

I ran off, hoping to survive in another village and escape trouble. But the fire gave the people of my village faith, and my aging slowed. I became immortal in pieces, sometimes falling asleep only to move between realms. Sometimes being powerless, and other times granting accidental miracles.

Being a teenager is awkward. Being a teenage goddess even more so.

But, my city grew and I aged, reaching my prime as the city ascended to its height of glory. And, as long as the city walls stayed safe and someone there vaguely believed in me, I could protect the city and remain forever beautiful and in my prime.

"Goddess! I need you!"

This time I got dressed and stepped between realms not into a brothel but into a bar brawl.

My curly-haired faithful man smiled apologetically from behind an overturned table. "I have run into a minor problem," he said as someone with an axe bellowed.

I waved my hand and slowed time. "A minor problem? You prayed for my rescuing hand for a minor problem?"

"Minor, but ah, life threatening." He had a winning smile.

Ah, good Me, this is why I put up with the reckless idiot. Not only did he believe in me with a steadfast certainty, but he amused me. "What kind of miracle are you looking for exactly?"

"If you could just hold time while I sneak out the back..." He was already standing, fingers lightly lifting someone's coins from their table as he edged toward the door.

"No theft," I ordered.

"I..." He dropped the coins and managed to look deeply wounded. "There's no rule about theft."

"I feel a new commandment coming on," I warned. "Right there. Tip of my tongue."

He cringed.

"Don't. Be. Stupid."

The faithful shouldn't glare at their chosen Goddess like sore losers, but this one did.

"When you cheat at cards and try to steal from one of the major gangs, it's considered very stupid to then use the powers of your Goddess and the miracle of an escape to clean them out."

"But, I have needs!"

"Try wooing a woman rather than buying them," I advised.

"I was thinking bread and cheese," he said, "but, yes, thank you. Ever since you showed up mid"—he coughed—"*show*, I've had trouble finding the will to engage in..." He waved a hand towards his hips. "...Things."

"Perhaps a life of celibacy is the life for you?"

"With this body?" He posed for me, slowly pirouetting to show an ideal masculine form. "It would be a crime against the Gods."

"Have you no shame?"

"None at all." His grin was unrepentant and shamelessly sexy.

I rolled my eyes and shook my head. "Bar brawls. Brothels. And whatever that thing was last month…"

"Last year!" he hastily corrected.

"Today is the first day of the new year." I glared and crossed my arms. "Last month was also last year."

"Isn't today a day of forgiveness?" he asked hopefully.

"I never said that."

"But you could," he pointed out. "You're the Goddess. You make the rules."

"And my rule is: don't be stupid. And don't expect me to bail you out of trouble because you've gotten into mischief."

"It's not mischief. This is…" He looked around the bar for inspiration. "…Financial restructuring of the local economy to help the poor."

"Theft?"

"Taxation."

I rolled my eyes as the prayerful thief hurried out of the bar. With a sigh I let time flow again and made my way across fallen bodies and past enraged bandits. "One glass of whatever's best."

The barkeep frowned at me. "Didn't see you come in, miss."

"That happens. No one looks for the gods in their lives unless they're desperate."

"True enough." She poured me a glass of something thick, brown, and spelling of incontinent horses.

I frowned at the mug in despair. "This is your best."

"Best in the whole city."

"Oh, Me."

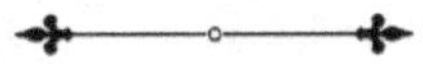

"Goddess, divine and forgiving. You have heard me before. In this, my hour of greatest need—"

"All right, all right." I stepped into the mortal world. "Why, in My name, are you being so flowery? Is this another broth—"

I stopped mid-sentence as a pair of hungry-eyed waifs stared up at me. They were wearing tattered, blood-stained rags and there was mud drying on their cheeks only cleaned by rivers of tears.

"These are not yours," I told the thief. "I made that expressly clear. No children until you asked for them."

The thief sighed. He was a little older now, matured and still handsome. But his eyes were filled with a weariness I'd never seen, a defeat, and his clothes, which had always been simple—and sometimes absent—were worn thin. "They are mine because I have taken care of them. Their parents are dead. The city is beset."

I felt a niggling pang of worry. The city had been conquered many times. It didn't matter to me. I was Goddess of the city, not the people in it. I wasn't counting the sparrows or noting when they fell. But now I felt some form of affection for the people of the city.

The thief gestured to the cave mouth. We were far removed from the city, which was odd, but I could see the wide plains where the forest once stood, the river swollen by spring rain, my city painted by fire and covered by the mourning weeds of ash. "All is falling, my Goddess. I didn't know what else to do."

"What miracle do you want?" I didn't know myself. The people in the city rarely prayed to me. They had no faith, and without faith any miracle I gave them would lie there unused. Godly magic wasn't like an enchanted lantern that flickered to life when someone said a magic word. My miracles required both my desire to grant the miracle and the recipient's desire to have a miracle.

The people of my city wanted no miracles.

I could keep the city standing. Clean the water. Save the walls. Ensure a plentiful harvest.

But I couldn't save the people.

For the first time in centuries, I felt sorrow that I couldn't do more.

The thief sighed heavily. "Could you give us safety?"

"Here? No. Not right now. But I can take you somewhere safe."

He nodded and a brief smile played across his lips. "Thank you, Goddess. I don't know if I've ever said that."

I smiled back at him sadly. "I'd rather hear you laughing merrily."

He looked away, trying to hide his pain from me.

"You do not need to protect me, little thief."

"We lost so much. So many people. I tried to tell them you could save us but…"

"…But prideful people have no time for thieves turned to prophets."

A ghost of a smile graced his lips. "Thief? Is that what you think of me?"

"You never told me your name."

"Ah, well, then I am a fool."

I touched his cheek, taking his worries and pain, leaving peace and health. "You are many things. Go with my blessing."

I opened a portal for them, letting them escape to another city where the God was generous and the people kind.

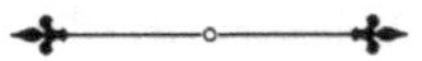

"Goddess, beloved above all else, I seek your presence. Goddess, are you there?"

It had been years since I'd heard his voice. I dressed with care, pulling on a shining white robe and arranging my hair into curls held by stars.

When I stepped into the mortal plane, we were on a stone balcony overlooking my city. Fires and smoke had been replaced by lights in windows and the music of a night market around the corner.

"Goddess." He bowed to me for the first time. He was dressed up as well, a clean chiton and a trimmed beard. He still looked impossibly young, but he must have been well into his third decade, if not older.

There was a small, round table laid for two with meat and wine and grapes.

"You seek my blessing?" He'd found a bridal bed at last, or perhaps at least the hope of one.

Something strange flowed through my veins, joy tinged by a sense of loss.

He smiled and shrugged. "Perhaps. I wished to speak with you. What do Goddesses eat?"

"Whatever we please."

"Ah, then perhaps this will suit you after all." He pulled a chair out for me and gestured for me to sit.

"You prepared me a meal? You didn't need to. I am well-fed by the city. Every food that falls to the ground is given to me."

The corner of his mouth pulled up in a wry grin. "I've been meaning to ask about that. Do you actually eat the food that falls in the dirt?"

"Of course not! But it would make a mortal sick if they ate it so it seemed fair to claim the fallen food as an of-fering to me. That way it isn't wasted, and at least some of you remember me." I sat, breathing in the aroma of warm spices. "Why this?"

He sat across from me. "Would you believe I missed seeing your face?"

"Aren't there statues of me?"

"They aren't a good likeness."

"There are mortal women who are quite beautiful, were they not good enough company?"

"I found myself comparing them to you." He pushed a grape across his plate. "I am in trouble, Goddess."

"That's not new." I took a bite of the meat. It was different than the last mortal food I'd had, but not at all unpleasant.

"I'm in love."

I nodded.

"I dream of her at night. Wake up longing for her in my arms. I grow hungry to hear her voice. I want her beside me. I would die for her touch."

I politely did not roll my eyes. "Yes.

Love. You said. I take it this woman does not return your affection."

"I'm not certain."

"I will not force a woman to love you," I said. "That isn't a miracle or a blessing, it's a curse. For both of you."

"I'm not asking you to force her," he said. "I'm asking for an answer."

I raised an eyebrow. "And you can't go ask this woman yourself."

He watched me intently. "I am asking. Goddess, do you love me?"

"Oh..." *Oh, Me*. He was asking me if I loved him. "Love you... Love you as a person in my city? Love you as the mortal you are? Or love you..."

"Do you love me as a woman loves a man?"

Oh, Me. I wish I had a way to blaspheme rather than cursing my own name. "I... I... I never thought about it."

"But you're here, every time I've called for you."

"Because I can hear you clearly!"

"You've protected me. Cared for me."

"Because that is the duty of a Goddess!"

"You've smiled at me. Laughed at me."

"Because you make me smile." I didn't know Goddesses could get flustered. But I was flustered, and well out of my depth. "I... I came to godhood in my youth. I've never... never..." I waved my hand between us.

"You've seen a naked man before." The familiar, lazy grin I knew well returned.

Now, I rolled my eyes. "Seeing you naked when you were barely grown hardly counts."

He leaned across the table. "I've improved with age."

I leaned in too. "I'm sure you have, but that doesn't matter. I'm not going to start having random dalliances with mortals. That sort of thing leads to no end of trouble."

"I'm not suggesting you have dalliances with random mortals."

"Good." Then the matter was settled. I could relax.

"I'm asking you to love me, and only me."

I sniffed. "Until when? Your mortal death? Do you wish to break the heart of a goddess?" Getting attached to mortals hurt. Their lives were so painfully short.

He laughed and smiled like the first night I'd manifested in the brothel. "My beloved Goddess, do you know how many years have passed since we last spoke?"

I looked around at the city for a clue. "Five, six years? Long enough to clean up the mess from the war."

He shook his head. "Do you know how many years have passed since we first met?"

"A decade or two I suppose."

"Centuries."

I stared at him. He didn't think he was lying, but he'd been nearly a full man the first time we'd met and he wasn't old yet. "No."

"Centuries have passed, Goddess. The orphans you saved last time I saw your face are all grandparents, great-grandparents. The men in the bar belonged to an empire that the sands washed away. The woman you saw that first time? Only I remember her name. Centuries have passed and I have barely aged."

"You're not a god. I'm very good at spotting these things."

"I'm not, but I am something other than mortal."

"How?"

He shrugged and drank his wine. "I thought nothing of it at first. I traveled. I wandered. I met other gods, although none like you. And I prayed to you. Your name on my lips every day. The thought of you with me every hour. Until, I suppose, some of your immortality granted me a longer life."

"I'm sorry. I never meant to curse you like that."

"It didn't bother me. I didn't think of it at all, until recently. I have new friends who are getting married. I made a stable life for myself. I stopped being a thief." He winked at me.

"Liar," I said with affection. "You'll always be a thief."

"An immortal thief." He held his goblet of wine to the starlight. "And what would be the thing a thief could steal that would keep his name alive for eternity?"

"I don't know." But I was willing to listen.

His dark brown eyes met mine. "Could I, possibly, steal the love of a goddess? Win her heart?" His gaze traveled down from my eyes to my lips and then lower with a hungry sigh. "Could I, Goddess?" He closed his eyes.

I stood. "Perhaps."

He looked at me. "Perhaps?"

"But not here. The setting is too formal. The mood is too somber. I am the Goddess, keeper of a marvelous city full of bright passions and joy. People offer me flowers, small weapons, and whatever food touches the ground. I am worshipped by sloshed beer and laughter and the thrum of music. This place, little thief, is not my temple."

His sexy smile returned. "Have it your way, Goddess. I'll be praying for you again soon."

Laughing, I faded into the celestial realm.

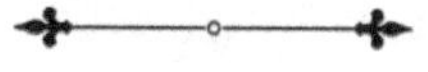

"Oh, Goddess! Goddess, I need you!" The prayer was sly and lusty, full of hidden thoughts and hunger.

I stepped out of my bath and wrapped myself in my garnet robe before I stepped into the mortal realm.

The thief lay enrobed in darkness, the golden glow of candle light embroidering his bare skin. "Goddess. I want you."

The prayer ignited my own hunger, a desire to play, and to touch, and to be touched.

"Goddess," he prayed, reaching for me, "Goddess who sees the city, who protects the strong and the weak, the maiden who loves our laughter and song—"

"Maiden?"

"Maiden." It was a challenge. "But not after tonight."

I hid a smile behind a mocking scowl.

"Goddess, bless my bridal bower."

He balanced himself on one elbow as he watched me walk closer. "Come and give me a night to remember."

"Only one?"

"Oh, no, Goddess. Every night. Every day. In the soft glow of the dawn and the falling calm of the twilight hours, Goddess, be with me. Let my tongue bring you joy. Let my hands find work to do."

I laughed. "Only you would make a hymn bawdy."

"Only you would make me beg for your caress. Come to me, Goddess."

"Oh, Me. You are a wicked one."

"There's no commandment against seducing my Goddess. I checked."

Laughter ringing through the night and filling the city with joy, I went to him, my prayerful supplicant. My thief. My lover.

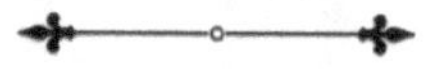

"Goddess! Oh, Goddess!"

The prayer echoed around the celestial realm as my lover fell back into our giant bed, sweat-slick and spent.

"Goddess, but that never gets old."

I kissed his cheek and rolled away, still perfectly in the prime of my life as he was in his. "Some of the people call me Mother Goddess now."

"Oh no. No, no, no." My lover shook his head. "Not for another century or two. We don't need children running around yet."

"I did promise you that if I blessed your bridal bed..." I teased.

His eyes went wide in fear. "Oh, Goddess, no! You said if I *wanted* that blessing. If I desired it. I have an immortal memory."

Running a hand along his leg, I gave his thigh a squeeze. "Not yet, but some day."

"Sweet Goddess, I would be a terrible father."

"You tend to the city well enough."

"That's different. Our own children would need to be raised here. We can't just hand them off to—" His eyes met mine. "Could we do that? Just hand them off to people? Give a couple wanting a child one of ours?"

"I don't know of any law against it."

He ran his hand along his jaw as he thought. "Huh. That might upset a number of major religions."

"I never started any of those. I never asked for worship or homilies, just common sense."

"And no thieving."

"I was trying to keep you out of trouble."

"You should have brought me home earlier."

"Are you questioning the wisdom of your Goddess?"

There was love in his eyes as he watched me change. "Never. I would never question my Goddess, except to ask her what she wants to do next."

How was it that I was the goddess and yet he was the one performing miracles? My quiet, boring days had been lost in the joy of his company. My worries and fears were soothed by his devoted presence beside me.

He raised his eyebrows as a know-ing smile crossed his face. "Goddess… what do you want to do?

"You," I said. "For the rest of eternity."

After discussing the idea of blasphemy with some religious friends I was struck by how annoying it would be for a god to be interrupted in their daily routines by someone calling their name.

Originally, the goddess was going to show up and punish the blasphemous young man, but then he started flirting and things snowballed from there.

In fact, it spun wildly out of control, didn't do at all what I'd expected, and wound up being one of my favorite short stories.

Read more by Liana Brooks!

ALL I WANT FOR CHRISTMAS IS A REAPER

THREE O'CLOCK ON A THURSDAY AFTERNOON IN APRIL, and I had an unplanned three-day weekend. In Chicago, my favorite city in the world. There were thunderheads gathering over Lake Michigan with the smell of rain in the air but, for now, downtown was a delightful playground of rushing cars, stressed commuters, and the bitter tears of lives I'd ruined with a pink slip.[1]

With nowhere in particular to be, I meandered, crossing Clark Street at the light to

---

[1] Technically this is a lie. Dulcie Waterhouse ruined her own life by embezzling from her firm and taking too many long lunch breaks buying macarons across town. The only tears were the tears of joy in her co-workers' eyes when they realized she was leaving for good. And there wasn't a pink slip. I con-vinced her to resign. I'm good like that.

reach a small city park with maple trees that wouldn't reach maturity in this century, a little playground with a sun shade, and a recycled rubber tire running track that crossed through the limited greenspace like a drunken snake trying to bite its own tail.

It was too early for school to be out and too late for lunch, which meant the park was populated by a muddy handful of toddlers, their attendant adults, and me. I kept to the outside track, crossing a stone footbridge over a shallow dirt ditch that might become a small pond if it rained. Tulips bobbed in the wind. The forsythia was out.

Little flowers and cheeky sparrows.

I enjoyed it for about four minutes before I could feel my brain scrabbling around like a trapped rat desperate for escape.

Natural vistas had that effect on me. I needed something to think about. A job to focus on. Numbers. Problems. City things.

At the sound of a jogger approaching, I stepped to the side so they could sweep past and catch the running track.

And sweep past he did. A gloriously muscular runner with olive-toned tan skin, a shock of silver-white hair shaved on the sides and long on top, a well-defined back and legs, and a black shirt sliding out of his waistband and dropping to the ground.

Well then.

It wasn't quite the young Miss Bennet dropping her gloves so a militia man could retrieve them for her, but it was possibly the twenty-first century equivalent. Even if it wasn't, it was only polite to collect the handsome man's shirt and return it to him.

I picked it up, shook off the dust and grass clippings, and held the sandalwood-scented shirt up for inspection. The owner was broad shouldered and the shirt was lean cut, meant to hug him and give everyone looking an excellent view of his well-defined muscles. Slightly more interesting was the word KILLER written across the front of the shirt in the font of the well-known horror brand, Slasher.

The jogger was a scary movie fan.

Not a lot to work with as openings went.

Scary movies weren't my cup of cocoa. No movies were, most days. Sitting still for hours on end listening to other people talk made me restless.

Perhaps it wasn't meant to be.

I folded the shirt neatly, and when I looked up the jogger was watching me from the bend of the running track only a few feet away, one white earbud hanging off his shoulder, the other still in his ear. He was younger than the white hair suggested, maybe twenties or early thirties, with dark brown—nearly black—eyes, high cheek-bones, a well-defined jaw line, and a sharp, straight nose. He looked exceptionally intense and unquantifiably captivating.

"Is that my shirt?" he asked in a deep voice as delicious as he was. I could listen to that man read the dictionary and I'd love every moment of it.

I held the shirt up, letting it unfurl over my dress. "I don't know, do you think it's mine?" I let him get a good look at me. Large, dark reds curls that looked a century out of date, a pink flower tucked behind my ear, pink lipstick, pretty smile, A-line green dress with pink flowers embroidered on it and a crinoline underneath for volume; I looked like a piece of walking history.

Twee. Sweet. Friendly.

Stupid.

I'd heard every verdict, but the dress

made me look fabulous and I loved bringing a pop of cheer to people's otherwise blighted lives.

"It'd look good on you. Killer." The corner of his mouth lifted in a sexy smile.

Oh. *No*. I did *not* like that.

Actually, I did, very much, but I knew where sexy smiles led. It would be hot nightclubs, wild parties, and then a trip to the suburbs as Mr. Sexy waxed lyrical about 'getting away from the city.' Pretty soon he'd be browsing baby name websites and talking about getting a dog.

No.

If a *Timberwolf Town*[2] werewolf couldn't tempt me, then a yappy little dog suitable for the suburbs didn't stand a chance.

I held the shirt to my shoulders and tried not to notice how good it smelled—sandalwood with an undertone of mint. The scent

---

[2] A paranormal-horror series from the mid 20s that centered around a hidden werewolf population and their unrivaled basketball team. I'm 90% certain that the ratings were due to the regular shower scenes.

was too light for a cologne—probably a soap. "It looks like my size, too." Assuming it was supposed to be worn halfway to my knees. Jogging, dark, and handsome was also tall, dark, and handsome.

"I'll let you borrow it some time." The man had dark, hungry eyes that promised to make my flirtation worth my time.

"Sure." That was never going to happen. I tossed the shirt to him. "Enjoy your run."

The smile turned to a smirk. "Enjoy the view." He secured the shirt to his waistband again and took off with a wink.

Confidence was always sexy, and I was very tempted to continue my little stroll around the park and see if the jogger wanted to join me for a post-workout snack some-where.

I was great at first dates. Lots of con-fidence and a big smile got me everything I wanted.

Second dates?

No one had tempted me enough to sche-dule a second date since college.

I glanced at the jogger again. *Maybe* no one had tempted me?

He looked familiar in that we–met–once–

in–passing sort of way.

My memory for names and faces was legendary, but I couldn't recall being introduced to him before.

It was going to bother me all afternoon if I didn't pursue it.

As if the office had a psychic link,[3] my phone rang, the quick staccato tattoo reserved for my boss. Work was there again, to rescue me from my worst impulses and save me from the kind of heartbreak ice cream couldn't fix.

"Hi, Amara." I moved toward the crosswalk, dodging a little green car that nearly swerved into me.

Chicago drivers. So charming.

There was a tiny community garden space across the street, a safe distance from the sexy jogger.

"Merri, I just heard the good word from Windy City Security, you've officially slayed the wicked witch of the upper west side. Did you break seven minutes?" Amara Rosa

---

[3] Or, let's be honest, a stopwatch to keep track of the betting on the Dulcie Waterhouse situation.

Park[4] was just as competitive as I was and she'd had my back in the office betting pool.

Sloan and Markham is *the* name in corporate accounting in Illinois. Amara is the head of the forensic accounting unit.

Really, we're a bunch of math nerds who read too many mystery novels and decided we'd grow up to fight white collar crime for a six-figure annual salary. And in the land of the nerds, I'm the big, brutal boss, the final, unconquerable hurdle.

"Six minutes," I said with a killer smile.[5]

"You make me so happy! Did Dulcie cry? I met her when I went in for the initial contact and…" Amara sighed. "Some people just *look* evil, you know?"

I pictured Dulcie Waterhouse in her gray pantsuit with a black silk shell under the jacket, two silver studs in each ear, a professional, asymmetrical cut for her dark brown hair, and dark red lipstick on a mouth pouring out more cuss words than could fit into a Monday morning commute when the

---

[4] Named for Amara Enyia and Rosa Parks, obviously.

[5] Ha ha, I'm so funny!

trains were down. "She didn't cry, but you may need to give the interns a bonus for reading my emails for the next few weeks."

"More death threats?" Amara sighed again. "What is it about you that attracts so much venom?"

"It's the job." And the fact that dressing like the lead singer from a retro throwback band made everyone underestimate me. What can I say? I have brains *and* beauty.

With a click of her tongue, Amara dismissed the disappointing news. "Well, done is done. I'll give the interns a heads up." There was a chime in the background. "Oh, and there's the first hit on social media. Want to hear it?"

"It's not like I'm going to look it up." I didn't do social media. Despite having an email assigned to me along with my social security number, I had the digital footprint of a ghost.

"The headline is 'Chicago's Infamous Grim Reaper Strikes Again.' Good job."

"I try my best."

Amara made a happy, purring sound. "Did you try your very best with Harry?"

"Harry?" I stopped in front of a bench.

"I'm drawing a blank."

"Junior executive in accounting?" Amara dangled the tidbit.

Mentally I flipped through a detailed list of junior accounting people. "Not ringing any bells."

"Henderson account?"

I shuddered.

"He sent you a gorgeous bouquet of day lilies—"

"He was telling me about how his parents were building a new house in Sugar Grove and how the commute was under thirty minutes to the city with the new high-speed trains."

There was a stunned silence and then Amara took a deep breath. "So…"

"So, thanks but no thanks? Give them to someone else."

"He left a note too."

Stupid man. But it was only polite to read the note and find some excuse for why I couldn't show up to Domestication Of The Wild Wifey 101. "Leave it on my desk. I'll deal with it when I get back to the office."

"About that…."

"You have another job for me before the weekend?" If there were gods who smiled fondly on math nerds, I would have prayed. Numbers and patterns were my favorite candy. A weekend sorting through someone else's finances as just as blissful as a bubble bath.

There was a hesitant little sigh, which meant Amara wasn't sold on the job but someone was begging. "This is an odd one. It's not the bosses calling, it's an employee, and she asked for you by name because she said you worked here, but she didn't seem to know what it is you do."

Weird. "The name?"

"Ellen Berry."

Someone else would have a hazy memory of a schoolyard friend who they'd met during a game of tag–turned–head–on–collision in kindergarten.

My memory was sharper than that, and off the top of my head I could rattle off all the major life events in Ellen's personal history up until she left for college in New York. We hadn't kept in touch mostly because I forgot people existed when I was working with math.

It was great for my bank account, but not for relationships.

"Merri?" Amara waited. "If I give you the address can you go over and see what's going on?"

"Sure. Where am I headed?"

"Cozy Studios—"

"Cozy as in Cozy TV with the candy-dipped romances?" Good grief. "Can I fire the writers for their poor plotlines?"

"Only if they're embezzling," Amara said. "Otherwise, give them the quick two-day special. A little workflow advice. A little hiring advice. And then get out of there, because we have the Oretega account to tackle next week."

Easy as mud pie in Mississippi. "Got it. In. Out. Tear-free."

"If you make it tear-free, I will personally buy you dinner anywhere in the city."

"I like expensive food," I warned.

"Cozy was just bought out by Slasher Corp," Amara reported with maybe just a soupçon of glee. "You're getting called in because Cozy is getting killed."

Keep reading! Head to
<u>www.inkprintpress.com/
lianabrooks/christmas/reaper/</u>
to buy your copy now!

ABOUT THE AUTHOR

LIANA BROOKS didn't set out to be a romance writer in disguise, but the clues are starting to add up as she experiments with romance in many forms: from sprawling space opera romances (the *Fleet of Malik* series) to the antics of a super-powered family as they each fall in love (the *Heroes and Villains* series), to the paranormal romances in the *All I Want For Christmas* series.

You can learn more about her and her books at www.LianaBrooks.com.

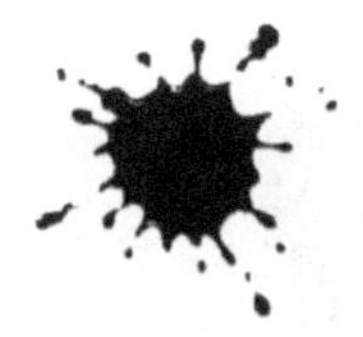

INKLETS

Collect them all! Released on the 1st and 15th of each month.

Dancer, Dreamer
Seer
LIANA BROOKS

As Time
Whirls Slowly
Past
AMY LAURENS

Far More
Satisfying
Than Hell
AMY LAURENS

Just
Another Day
In Hell
LIANA BROOKS

Moon AND
Morning
AMY LAURENS

Some
Impropriety
Expected
AMY LAURENS

NEON SNOW
LIANA BROOKS

Reincarnation
LIANA BROOKS

More Than
Mushrooms
AMY LAURENS

DOUBLE ISSUE
INKLET #092
How To Make A Star
& The World Ended
LIANA BROOKS

INKLET #093
CAUGHT
IN THE ACT
AMY LAURENS

INKLET #094
ANUBIS
Has Sent You
Six Souls
LIANA BROOKS

INKLET #095
PRAYER TO A
GODDESS
LIANA BROOKS

INKLET #096
Love In The
Time Of Corona
AMY LAURENS

INKLET #097
RECRUITMENT
AMY LAURENS

INKLET #098
IDENTITY
Theft 101
LIANA BROOKS

INKLET #099
Curses
With Benefits
AMY LAURENS

INKLET #100
NECROMANCER
TROUBLES
LIANA BROOKS